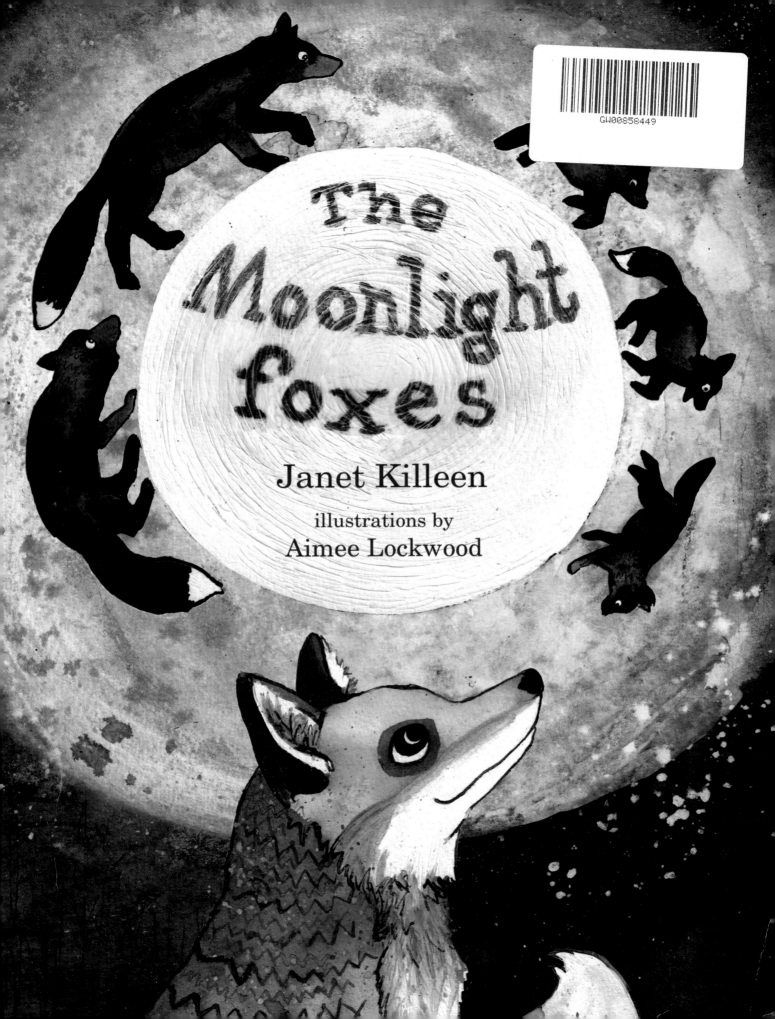

The Moonlight Foxes

Janet Killeen

illustrations by
Aimee Lockwood

AuthorHouse™ LLC
1663 Liberty Drive
Bloomington, IN 47403
www.authorhouse.com
Phone: 1-800-839-8640

Published by AuthorHouse 09/23/2013

ISBN: 978-1-4918-7940-5 (sc)
ISBN: 978-1-4918-7941-2 (e)

Printed in Canada by Friesens
December 2013
90881

authorHOUSE®

For Daniel and Rachel
(who owned the flip flops),
and Bethan and Philip, with love.

There are Foxes at the Bottom of the Garden

At the very bottom of Mrs McNickleson's garden, under the shed, lives a family of foxes. Father Reginald, Mother Rita and their four cubs: Rosie, Rupert, Roberta and Roger. This is the family that you can hear at night going 'Yip, yip, yip' to the moon.

There are foxes at the bottom of the garden. But how did they get there? Where did they come from?

At the Very Beginning...

Reginald and Rita lived, long ago, long before their fox cub babies were born, in woods that grew at the edge of the Golf Course on the very outskirts of The Big City. They lived there happily, raiding the dustbins of the Golf Club for the remains of the Golfers' dinners and making do with beetles and snails when the Club closed down in winter.

Sometimes they ran to the fields owned by Mr Tompkins the farmer, got through a gap in the hedge and into the farmyard. If they were very quick they might catch a hen full of feathers and squawking, but not often. Mostly they met the farmyard cat, huge and fierce with blazing green eyes and they didn't stop to   argue. They would tip-toe away, shaking their hips as they went and swishing their tails. 'Beetles again tonight, dear', said Rita and they sighed and   scrunched side by side.

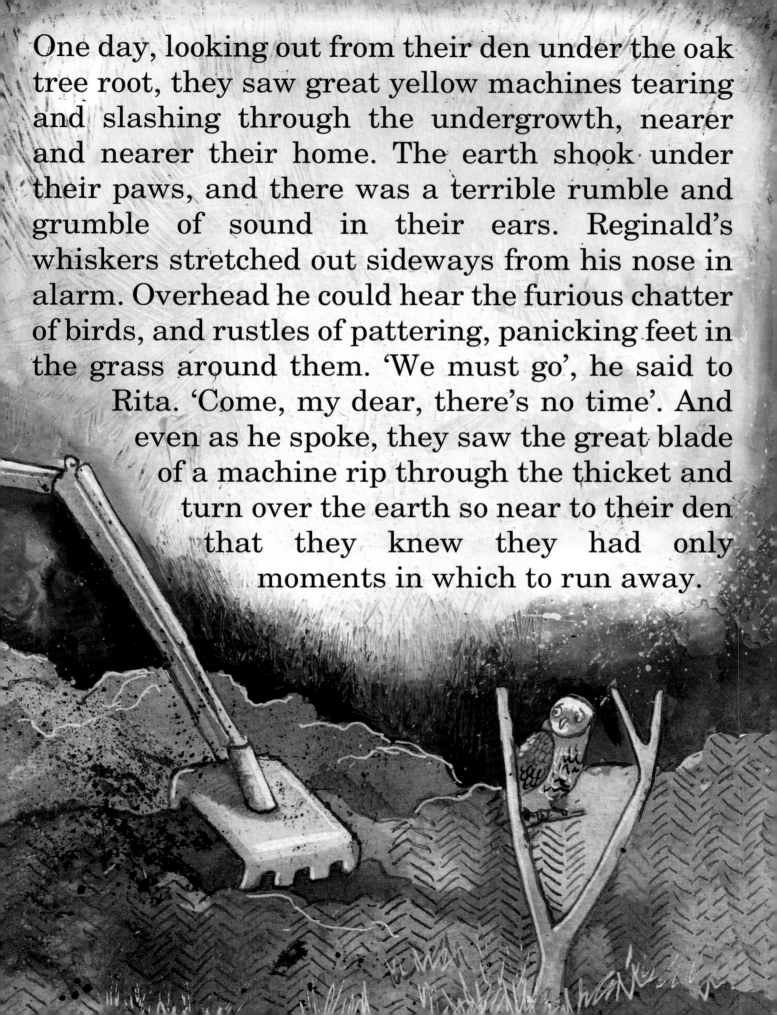

One day, looking out from their den under the oak tree root, they saw great yellow machines tearing and slashing through the undergrowth, nearer and nearer their home. The earth shook under their paws, and there was a terrible rumble and grumble of sound in their ears. Reginald's whiskers stretched out sideways from his nose in alarm. Overhead he could hear the furious chatter of birds, and rustles of pattering, panicking feet in the grass around them. 'We must go', he said to Rita. 'Come, my dear, there's no time'. And even as he spoke, they saw the great blade of a machine rip through the thicket and turn over the earth so near to their den that they knew they had only moments in which to run away.

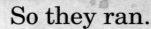

Run for Your Life

So they ran.

They ran through the wood and over the green mounds and sandpits of the Golf Course, dodging the diamond-socked legs of the golfers and leaving paw-prints in the sand.

They ran under the gate, and then in a blare of car horns, across the road, to arrive gasping with terror and shock in the garden of a large house, with three cars on the drive.

They could hardly pause for breath before they ran again, fleeing from the family that burst from the front door with two large dogs on leads. The dogs, seeing the flicker of russet and the white tips of their tails and smelling the scent of fox, set up a loud barking and howling, straining at their leads and pawing the air with their front legs. Reginald longed to turn back and make rude remarks but Rita snapped, 'Come on!' in a voice that he knew must be obeyed.

So they ran together, streaks of red-brown fox, so fast that only a wise cat and a child looking out of the window together saw them dash across the lawn and scrabble under the hedge.

Then, on and on, through streets and gardens for miles until the memory of that terrifying earth-ripping sound and the uprooted trees and bushes was far behind them. Only then, in a quiet corner of a churchyard, did they dare to stop. They lay panting, huddled with fear and shock. Later, they licked their sore paws, and limped into the bushes and nettles that grew by the wall, and, too tired to hunt for food, slept while the moon rose and all the creatures of the churchyard whispered about them.

Lost in the City

When night fell, and the orange street lamps turned the road into a zigzag of shadows, they set off, keeping close to the hedges and walls of the street, and waiting until some instinct told them that they had found a new home and could live in safety.... the safety of the space that they found in the early hours of the morning, underneath Mrs McNickleson's shed.

For a long time, Reginald and Rita were very careful to come out from their hiding place only at night. At first, the sounds of traffic from the busy main road at the end of their street roared in their ears, and the weird wailings of sirens terrified them. There were strange sounds too all around them. Water gushed down drainpipes, but they could not see a stream. Dogs barked. There were shouts and squeals from children at play. And Mrs McNickleson would fling open her back door at 7.30 every morning and call to her cat. She was a large lady with long arms and a booming voice, and the way she rattled the spoon against the tin of Cat Food sounded very fierce.

Achilty the Cat

'Achilty! Achilty!' Mrs McNickleson would cry, and Achilty would stroll from his secret warm place in a neighbour's garage and rub his whiskers round Mrs McNickleson's ankles in devotion.

He was a smug, fluffed-up, roly-poly creature of mottled co-
lours and a tail that waved from side to side with a stately
swish as he strolled up the garden path. Out came the tin, the
spoon and the bowl, and Achilty swooned over his food and
staggered away to rest. Hiding under the shed, the two foxes
watched in horror each day until they realised that he was so
lazy and so out of condition that he had chosen to ignore
them. They saw his narrowed green eyes looking directly at
them. Then he chose to turn his back and go and
flop down in a patch of sunlight and pant gently
and digest his breakfast. Every morning Reginald and Rita watched hopefully, but there was
never a scrap
left in his
large bowl.

The Cubs are Born

One day, many weeks after they had arrived and settled into the neighbourhood, Reginald and Rita became the proud parents of four fox cubs: Rosie, Rupert, Roberta and Roger. From the very beginning, as soon as they could stagger to their paws and twitch their whiskers, these four cubs were full of mischief. They danced in the moonlight, pattering with their naughty feet on the dustbins so that they made ranki-tank music on the tin lids. They crept over fences and stole clothes from the line, bringing home Shantelle's Brownie uniform to dress-up in.

Another night they chewed Daniel and Rachel's flip-flops which gave them terrible pains in their stomachs. 'Quite right too,' said their Mother and told them to go and eat grass to deal with the strange wind that chased up and down their insides. 'That will teach you. A fox needs to know what is good and right to eat. And flip-flops do not come on the menu.' Some nights they ran races in the middle of the lawn, daring each other to go closer and closer to Achilty the cat, who watched them from the garage door with huge, green, moonlit eyes.

Lessons that Must be Learned

One clear night, when he felt that they were old enough to listen and learn sensibly, Father Reginald took them for a long walk to the very end of the street and told them to sit down. They watched him, puzzled, their heads tilted on one side, their pink tongues slipping in and out of their mouths.

'This is your home,' he said to them, looking at each of them carefully.

'Listen to me, Roger. Sit up straight, Rosie. Stop shuffling and scratching all of you. You need to know your history. How your Mother and I came here from the dreadful dangers of the far wood. How we ran and ran to find a place to live so that when you were born you could be safe.'

Then he told them the story of that terrible day and night, and the adventure of their escape from everything that they had known to come to live in the streets of a town, in a garden, under a shed.

'This is the furthest you must ever travel,' he said, marking a line on the pavement with his paw. 'And that is the way home. You must know how to run across the road safely, slip like a shadow down the street, jump the gate, crawl under the hedge and find your way back to the shed. You can play in the moonlight, but you need to know how to hide in the shadows too.

Always remember the way to run home and be safe. Always remember the journey that your brave Mother and I took.' He paused, and four silent fox cubs realised that he was very serious and that they must listen and remember. 'One day you will teach your cubs how they can safely be moonlight foxes. How you can dance and howl to the moon, but stay carefully hidden in the daylight.' He looked round and saw the big eyes of his cubs watching him, and managing to concentrate even though a particularly juicy beetle was walking in front of their noses. 'Now, run!' he said. 'Across the road, down the street, over the gate, under the hedge and home! And never forget!' Four russet streaks of fox cub chased each other home.

For a very short time, four serious little foxes lay panting in the shelter of Mrs McNickleson's shed. Just for a moment. Then they all wriggled said, 'Oh Dad, that's so heavy!' And out they ran to jump up and down and squeal 'yip, yip, yip!' as they chased each other under the cool white light of the moon.

Adventures to Remember

As time went on, Rosie and Rupert, Roberta and Roger had more adventures of their own. One night Rupert climbed too far into a great grey wheelie bin in search of the lamb bones from Mr Yianni's barbecue and fell down to the bottom. His sisters heard him and came to his rescue, whispering instructions to Roger to prop up the lid so that he could jump out, bruised and shivering and smelling of garlic, lemon and herbs. 'Of course I wasn't scared,' he said and ran round and round and round in the garden to prove it.

Another time the four cubs lay in wait for Achilty's breakfast and stole it as soon as Mrs McNickleson had turned her back and gone into the kitchen door.

Achilty set up such a wailing and hissing that she came back out straight away, and they only just managed to run under the shed and lie there grinning and smacking their chops – until Mrs McNickleson got a broom and started to push it towards their den. Four pairs of eyes watched in horror as the broom came nearer and nearer to their safe, snug corner called home. Reginald and Rita had very strong words to say to them about that!

The adventures of the four cubs are full of fun and naughtiness. They laugh together as only fox cubs can, snickering and sniggering, and rolling over and over with all four paws in the air. One day they would tell their own cubs about the wild adventures of their young days, but they knew that their adventures were nothing like the serious story of their parents' escape. And that, too, is the story they will pass on to their cubs.

So they never forget.

The foxes at the bottom of the garden remember how to run for their lives. And sometimes they look up at the white and grey old moon and think of the story of Reginald and Rita. And that makes them prance and dance with great pride, flickering in and out of the moonlight and shadows of the garden.

About the Illustrator

AIMEE LOCKWOOD is an illustrator inspired by animals, by cities, by the sea and by stories. She likes nothing better than sitting in a cafe in her native Edinburgh, drawing the world going by. To see more of her work visit her website: www.aimeelockwood.c.uk

About the Author

JANET KILLEEN lives in South London. A retired teacher, she has published collections of short stories for adults as well as writing for children. She believes children can be empowered with language, and develop imagination, humour and empathy through stories they enjoy. Her first story, 'The Barking Cat' is already published by Authorhouse and will be followed by 'Roundabout Rabbits' and 'Small Bear' before Christmas 2013. To find out about her adult stories visit her website, www.janetkilleen.com